King & Kayla

and the Case of the
Gold Ring

Written by
Dori Hillestad Butler

Illustrated by
Nancy Meyers

PEACHTREE
ATLANTA

For Nancy, my FAVORITE illustrator!

—D. H. B.

For Danny with love

—N. M.

Published by
PEACHTREE PUBLISHING COMPANY INC.
1700 Chattahoochee Avenue
Atlanta, Georgia 30318-2112
www.peachtree-online.com

Text © 2021 by Dori Hillestad Butler
Illustrations © 2021 by Nancy Meyers

Edited Kathy Landwehr
Design and composition by Adela Pons

The illustrations were drawn in pencil, with color added digitally.

Printed in November 2020 by Toppan Leefung in China
10 9 8 7 6 5 4 3 2 1 (hardcover)
10 9 8 7 6 5 4 3 2 1 (trade paperback)

First Edition
HC ISBN 978-1-68263-207-9
PB ISBN 978-1-68263-208-6

Cataloging-in-Publication Data is available from the Library of Congress.

Contents

Chapter One 4
Playing in the Snow

Chapter Two..16
Retracing Our Steps

Chapter Three..26
Back Outside!

Chapter Four..34
Where's That Crow?

Chapter Five 40
Something Shiny

Chapter One

Playing in the Snow

Hello!

My name is King. I'm a dog. This is Kayla. She is my human.

Kayla, Mason, and I are playing in the snow. I LOVE the snow. It's my favorite thing!

"Hey, everyone!" says a girl at the
fence. "Come see what I have!"

It's Asia! I haven't seen her in
eleventy-five days!

Guess what? She's got liver treats! I
LOVE liver treats. They're my favorite
food!

"King! No jump," Kayla says.

"What do you have, Asia?" Mason asks.

"She has liver treats," I say. "I don't see them, but I smell them."

Asia takes off her glove. "A gold ring," she says. "It's very special because it was my grandma's when she was my age."

"It's pretty," Kayla says.

"And shiny," I say. "Can I have a liver treat?"

"Come play with us," Mason says to Asia.

"Okay," Asia says.

Kayla, Mason, and Asia throw
snowballs.

I chase a crow away.

"Brr! I'm getting cold," Asia says.

"Me too," Kayla says. "Let's go inside. My mom will make us hot chocolate with marshmallows."

I LOVE marshmallows. They're my favorite food!

Kayla, Mason, and Asia take off their coats, hats, and gloves. Mom puts the wet clothes in the dryer.

Then Kayla, Mason, and Asia wash their hands.

Finally, it's SNACK TIME!

After snack time, we watch some TV.

I still smell those liver treats.

All of a sudden, Asia cries out,

"My gold ring! It's gone!"

Chapter Two

Retracing Our Steps

"What happened to my ring?" Asia asks.

"When did you last see it?" Kayla asks.

"I had it when I got here," Asia says. "Where could it be?"

"Maybe it fell off while we were watching TV," Mason says.

We search the couch.
We search the pillows.
We search the floor.

No ring.

"Let's retrace our steps," Kayla says.

"We had a snack before we watched TV," Asia says.

"So maybe it's in the kitchen," Mason says.

I LOVE the kitchen. It's my favorite room!

Look! There are graham cracker
crumbs on the kitchen floor. I LOVE
graham crackers. They're my favorite
food!

"Your ring isn't on the table," Kayla says.

Asia looks under the table. "Your dog is under here," she tells Kayla. "And he's licking his lips. Maybe he ate my ring."

"I don't think he'd do that," Kayla says.

"Are you sure?" Asia asks. "Our dog ate a
penny once."

Kayla opens my mouth. "I hope he didn't
eat it," she says.

"I didn't," I say. But Kayla doesn't
understand me.

"Let's keep looking," Kayla says. "What did we do before we had our snack?"

I know! We played outside! I LOVE to play outside. It's my favorite thing!

I run to the door.

No one follows me.

"We washed our hands before we had our snack," Asia says.

"Maybe your ring went down the drain," Mason says.

"Can we get it out?" Asia asks.

Mom takes the drain apart. "I'm sorry, Asia," she says. "I don't see your ring in here."

"Then there's only one other place it could be," Mason says.

"OUTSIDE!" I say.

Chapter Three

Back Outside!

Kayla, Mason, and Asia get their coats, hats, and gloves from the dryer. Then we all go OUTSIDE!

"We'll never find my ring out here," Asia says.

"Not if we don't look," Kayla says.

We search the snow fort. We search the
pile of snowballs. No ring.

There's that crow again. I chase him away.

"King! Stop bothering that crow!" Kayla says.

Wait a minute. Crows like shiny things.
Asia's ring is shiny. Did the crow take
her ring?

"Come on, everyone," Kayla says. "Let's
go back inside. You too, King!"

Kayla grabs a notebook and pencil. "Let's make a list of everything we *know* about this case."

1. Asia's ring is missing.

2. It was on her finger when she came over.

3. We didn't find it in the cushions, on the table, in the drain, or outside.

If I could write, I would add this to Kayla's list of things we *know*:

There's a crow outside.

Crows like shiny things.

"Now, let's make a list of what we *don't know* about this case," Kayla says.

1. Did we miss Asia's ring in our search?

2. Is it someplace we haven't looked?

3. Did King eat it?

If I could write, I would add this to Kayla's list of things we *don't know*:

"Now we need a *plan*," Kayla says.

I have a plan:

Chapter Four

Where's That Crow?

I scratch at the door. "Let me out! Let me out!" I say.

"You were just outside," Kayla tells me.

"I need to go out again," I say. "I need to find the crow's nest."

"Maybe you should let him out," Mason says. "If he ate Asia's ring, we want it to come out the other end."

Asia groans.

Kayla opens the door and I run outside.

Now where's that crow? Sniff...sniff...

Where's that crow's *nest*? Sniff...sniff...

"SQUAWK!!!!"

"There you are!" I say. "Did you take
  Asia's ring?"

"If I did, it's mine,"
the crow says.
"Finders keepers!"

He flies over our
fence.

I won't let him get away
with this. I back up so
I can get a running start
and...

Kayla grabs my collar. "Oh, no you don't," she says.

"But...that crow—" I try and explain.

Kayla brings me inside. "We're trying to solve a case," she says.

"I know. I'm trying to solve it, too!" I say. "We have to follow that crow! We have to find his nest!"

Kayla sighs. "If you won't stop barking, you'll have to stay in the laundry room," she says.

She leaves the room and closes the door.

Chapter Five

Something Shiny

I have to get out of here. I have to help Kayla solve this case. And I'd still like one or five of Asia's liver treats.

I pace back and forth. I look out the window. I pace back and forth again.

Wait a minute. There's something shiny inside the dryer.

"HEY!" I yell. "THERE'S SOMETHING SHINY INSIDE THE DRYER!"

I scratch at the dryer door. I can't get
it open.

Kayla comes back. "Why are you
barking? Why are you scratching?"
she asks.

"Come see," I say.

She comes closer. She looks inside the
dryer.

"Oh, I get it," she says, patting my
head. "Good boy, King!"

"Asia! Mason! Come here," Kayla calls. She opens the dryer door.

"My gold ring!" Asia cries. "Thank you! Thank you!" She grabs the ring and puts it back on her finger.

"How did you know it was in there?"
Mason asks.

"I had a little help from King," Kayla
says. "I bet the ring came off inside
Asia's glove when we were playing.
And then it probably fell out of the
glove in the dryer."

"Your dog is really smart," Asia says.

"I know," Kayla says.

And *I* know that Asia still has those treats!

"Please can I have a treat?" I beg.

"Can I give your dog a treat?" Asia asks.

"Yes! Yes, you can!" I say.

"Okay," Kayla says.

Asia reaches into her pocket and pulls out a liver treat. I LOVE liver treats. They're my favorite food!"

The End

Oh, boy! I LOVE books.
They're my favorite things!
And everyone loves King and Kayla!

"...a great introduction to mysteries, gathering facts, and analytical thinking for an unusually young set."
—*Booklist*

"A perfect option for newly independent readers ready to start transitioning from easy readers to beginning chapter books."—*School Library Journal*

"Readers will connect with this charmingly misunderstood pup (along with his exasperated howls, excited tail wagging, and sheepish grins)." —*Kirkus Reviews*

King & Kayla and the Case of the Missing Dog Treats

HC: 978-1-56145-877-6
PB: 978-1-68263-015-0

King & Kayla and the Case of the Lost Tooth

HC: 978-1-56145-880-6
PB: 978-1-68263-018-1

King & Kayla and the Case of the Secret Code

HC: 978-1-56145-878-3
PB: 978-1-68263-016-7

King & Kayla and the Case of Found Fred

HC: 978-1-68263-052-5
PB: 978-1-68263-053-2

King & Kayla and the Case of the Mysterious Mouse

HC: 978-1-56145-879-0
PB: 978-1-68263-017-4

King & Kayla and the Case of the Unhappy Neighbor

HC: : 978-1-68263-055-6
PB: 978-1-68263-056-3